Thank you to the generous team who gave their time and talents to make this book possible:

Author
Elizabeth Taylor

Illustrators
Haile Lijam and Beth Molla

Creative Directors
Caroline Kurtz, Jane Kurtz, and Kenny Rasmussen

Translator
Amlaku B. Eshetie

Designer
Jordy Farrell and Beth Crow

Ready Set Go Books, an Open Hearts Big Dreams Project

Special thanks to Ethiopia Reads donors and staff for
believing in this project and helping get it started-- and
for arranging printing, distribution, and training in Ethiopia.

08/20/19

Let's Go!

ኑ እንሂድ!

English and Amharic

Let's go to the city.

ወደ ከተማ እንሂድ።

We can ride in a train.

በባቡር ተሳፍረን መሄድ እንችላለን።

Let's go to the market.

ወደ ገብያ እንሂድ።

We can ride on a mule.

በቅሎ ጋልበን መሄድ እንችላለን።

Let's go to the mosque.

ወደ መስጊድ
እንሂድ።

We can ride in a bajaj.

በባጃጅ መሄድ እንችላለን።

Let's go to the
countryside.

ወደ ገጠር
እንሂድ።

We can ride in a bus.

በአውቶብስ ተሳፍረን መሄድ እንችላለን።

Let's go someplace
far away.

ወደሆነ ሩቅ ቦታ እንሂድ።

We can ride in an airplane.

በአውሮፕላን ተሳፍረን መሄድ እንችላለን።

Let's go to
the clinic.

ወደ ክሊኒክ
እንሂድ።

We can ride on a horse and cart.

በፈረስ ጋሪ መሄድ እንችላለን።

Let's go to
the cafe.

ወደ ካፌ እንሂድ።

We can ride on a motorcycle.

በሞተር ብስክሌት መሄድ እንችላለን።

ወደ ከተማ
እንሂድ።

Let's go to
the town.

We can ride in a taxi.

በታክሲ ተሳፍረን መሄድ እንችላለን።

Let's go to
the school.

ወደ ትምህርት
ቤት እንሂድ።

We can ride on a bicycle.

በብስክሌት መሄድ እንችላለን።

Let's go to the church.

ወደ ቤተክርስቲያን
እንሂድ።

We can ride in a car.

በቤት መኪና መሄድ እንችላለን።

Where will we go? How will we get there?

ወዴት እንሂድ? በምን እንሄዳለን?

Come!
Let's go!

ኑ እንሂድ!

About The Story

In Ethiopia, people often walk or run to get to where they need to go. But many types of transportation also carry people from one place to another. Planes fly high, donkeys clomp by, bajajs zip around, motorcycles weave through traffic, and (in more and more places) trains travel on rails. Recently, the addition of a fully electrified cross border railway line--the first of its kind on the continent of Africa—has made travel smoother between Addis Ababa and the Red Sea port of Djibouti. The initial emphasis was on carrying goods (like containers) more efficiently for businesses, but passenger trains followed. https://www.bbc.com/news/world-africa-37562177

One traveler writes, "The trip is fun, the landscape changing is fabulous, you can see the villages, herds of goats and sheep, camels and monkeys."

About the Author

Elizabeth Spor Taylor is an international literacy specialist who served as writer and editor of English learning materials for Ethiopian students. She has traveled to Ethiopia eleven times visiting schools and working collaboratively with Ethiopian educators throughout the country. Elizabeth became familiar with the successes of

Ethiopia Reads while touring sponsored libraries in various regions of Ethiopia. Her expertise is in primary grades literacy relative to native English speakers as well as English Speakers of Other Languages. She is a contributing member of the Book Centered Learning Committee for Ethiopia Reads and supports the advancement of English skills within the refugee population in Cleveland, Ohio.

Elizabeth among English for Ethiopia textbooks as they are printed and assembled in Addis Ababa.

About The Illustrators

Bethelhem (Beth Molla) is a 2016 graduate of Ale school of fine arts and design. Born and raised in Addis Ababa, Ethiopia, she has been interested in art for quite a while. After graduating from Addis Ababa University, she opened her own small company called Dede Studio, a place for creative digital arts, illustrations, animation and related works.

Beth has won several art competitions locally and internationally. She has participated in different kinds of group exhibitions for the past years, and she plans to make her first solo art exhibition soon. Her illustrations are bright because she is a color fanatic. She enjoys making comics that speak her mind. Making fun characters for children is also her favorite thing to do since she wants to contribute something valuable for children using stylized illustrations. Beth believes that this kind of art will help children be interested in reading books.

****

Born and raised in Ethiopia, Haile Lijam is an accomplished artist who illustrates narrative and informational books to enhance student learning.

About Ready Set Go Books

Reading has the power to change lives, but many children and adults in Ethiopia cannot read. One reason is that Ethiopia has very few books in local languages to give people a chance to practice reading. Ready Set Go books wants to close that gap and open a world of ideas and possibilities for kids and their communities.

When you buy a Ready Set Go book, you provide critical funding to create and distribute more books.

Learn more at: http://openheartsbigdreams.org/book-project/

About Ethiopia Reads

Ethiopia Reads was started by volunteers in places like Grand Forks, North Dakota; Denver, Colorado; San Francisco, California; and Washington D.C. who wanted to give the gift of reading to more kids in Ethiopia. One of the founders, Jane Kurtz, learned to read in Ethiopia where she spent most of her childhood and where the circle of life has come around to bring her Ethiopian-American grandchildren. As a children's book author, Jane is the driving force behind Ready Set Go Books - working to create the books that inspire those just learning to read.

About Open Hearts Big Dreams

Open Hearts Big Dreams began as a volunteer organization, led by Ellenore Angelidis in Seattle, Washington, to provide sustainable funding and strategic support to Ethiopia reads, collaborating with Jane Kurtz. OHBD has now grown to be its own nonprofit organization supporting literacy, art, and technology for young people in Ethiopia.

Ellenore comes from a family of teachers who believe education is a human right, and opportunity should not depend on your birthplace. And as the adoptive mother of a little girl who was born in Ethiopia and learned to read in the U.S., as well as an aspiring author, she finds the chance to positively impact literacy hugely compelling!

About the Language

Amharic is a Semetic language -- in fact, the world's second-most widely spoken Semetic language, after Arabic. Starting in the 12th century, it became the Ethiopian language that was used in official transactions and schools and became widely spoken all over Ethiopia. It's written with its own characters, over 260 of them. Eritrea and Ethiopia share this alphabet, and they are the only countries in Africa to develop a writing system centuries ago that is still in use today!

About the Translation

Translation is currently being coordinated by a volunteer, Amlaku Bikss Eshetie who has a BA degree in Foreign Languages & Literature, an MA in Teaching English as a Foreign Language, and PhD courses in Applied Linguistics and Communication, all at Addis Ababa University. He taught English from elementary through university levels and is currently a passionate and experienced English-Amharic translator. As a father of three, he also has a special interest in child literacy and development. He can be reached at: khaabba_ils@protonmail.com

Find more Ready Set Go Books on Amazon.com

To view all available titles, search "Ready Set Go Ethiopia" or scan QR code

 Chaos

 Talk Talk Turtle

 The Glory of Gondar

 We Can Stop the Lion

 Not Ready!

 Fifty Lemons

Made in the USA
Lexington, KY
13 December 2019